KT-497-669

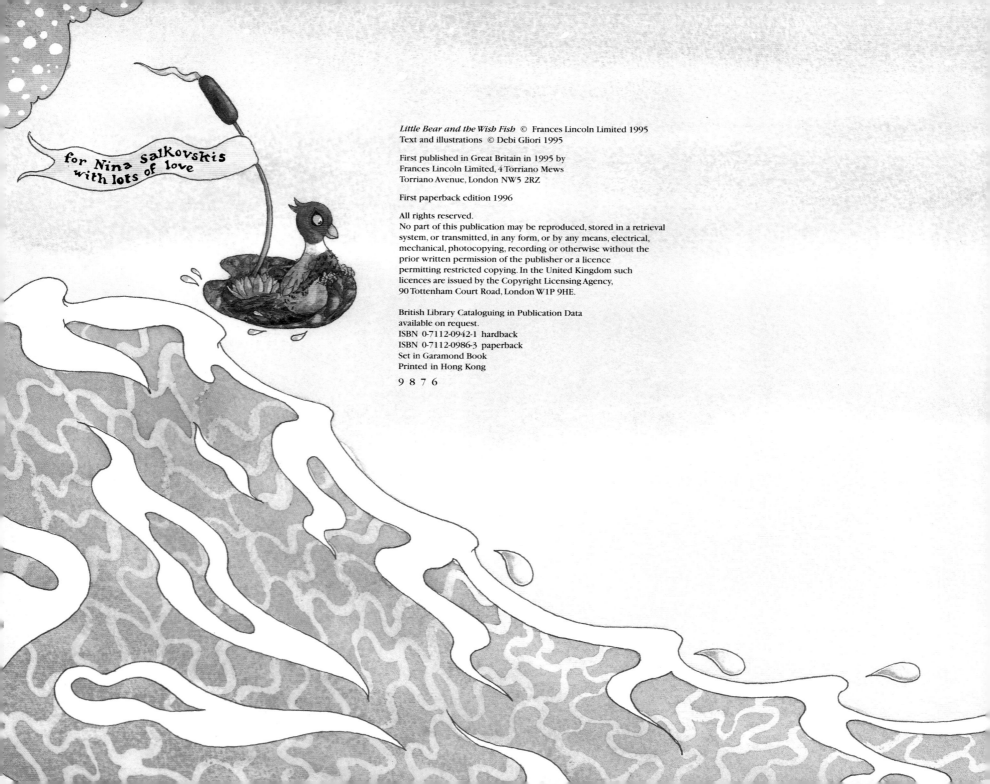

for Nina Salkovskis
with lots of love

Little Bear and the Wish Fish © Frances Lincoln Limited 1995
Text and illustrations © Debi Gliori 1995

First published in Great Britain in 1995 by
Frances Lincoln Limited, 4 Torriano Mews
Torriano Avenue, London NW5 2RZ

First paperback edition 1996

All rights reserved.
No part of this publication may be reproduced, stored in a retrieval
system, or transmitted, in any form, or by any means, electrical,
mechanical, photocopying, recording or otherwise without the
prior written permission of the publisher or a licence
permitting restricted copying. In the United Kingdom such
licences are issued by the Copyright Licensing Agency,
90 Tottenham Court Road, London W1P 9HE.

British Library Cataloguing in Publication Data
available on request.
ISBN 0-7112-0942-1 hardback
ISBN 0-7112-0986-3 paperback
Set in Garamond Book
Printed in Hong Kong

9 8 7 6

Debi Gliori studied illustration and design at Edinburgh College of Art.
Among her many successful picture books is the award-winning Mr Bear series (Orchard).
Mr Bear to the Rescue won the 1997 Childrens Book Award and *Mr Bear's New Baby*
was the winner of the Scottish Arts Council Children's Book Award 2000. In 2001
she published *Pure Dead Magic* (Doubleday), her first novel for children.
Debi lives with her family just outside Edinburgh.

Little Bear and the Wish Fish

DEBI GLIORI

FRANCES LINCOLN

The bears of Papana River Valley led a charmed life.
When it was raining, they fished.
When it was snowing, they hunted.
When the sun shone, they sunbathed.
Life was just peachy.

And yet ... for the bears, the weather was
never quite right.
They complained when it rained, "It's too wet!"
They complained when it snowed, "It's too cold!"
They even complained when the sun came out, "It's too hot!"

The weather-makers were not amused.
The Raindancer, the Sunblazer and the Snowmaker
were doing their best to make perfect weather for bears,
but all they heard in return were loud moans and groans.

So the Raindancer, the Sunblazer
and the Snowmaker decided to teach
those bears a lesson they would
never forget.
First, they caught a fish upstream
of the bear cave.

Next, they gave the fish
the power to grant wishes.
Last of all, they released
the fish, slippety slithery,
back into the river
near the bear cave.

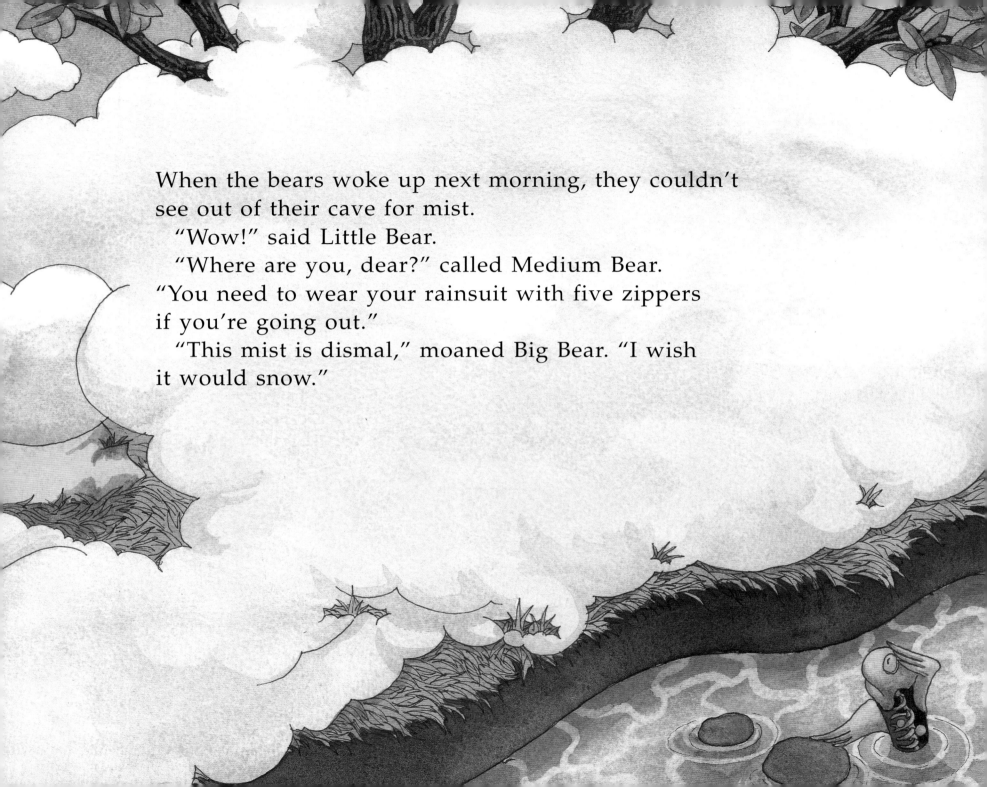

When the bears woke up next morning, they couldn't
see out of their cave for mist.

"Wow!" said Little Bear.

"Where are you, dear?" called Medium Bear.
"You need to wear your rainsuit with five zippers
if you're going out."

"This mist is dismal," moaned Big Bear. "I wish
it would snow."

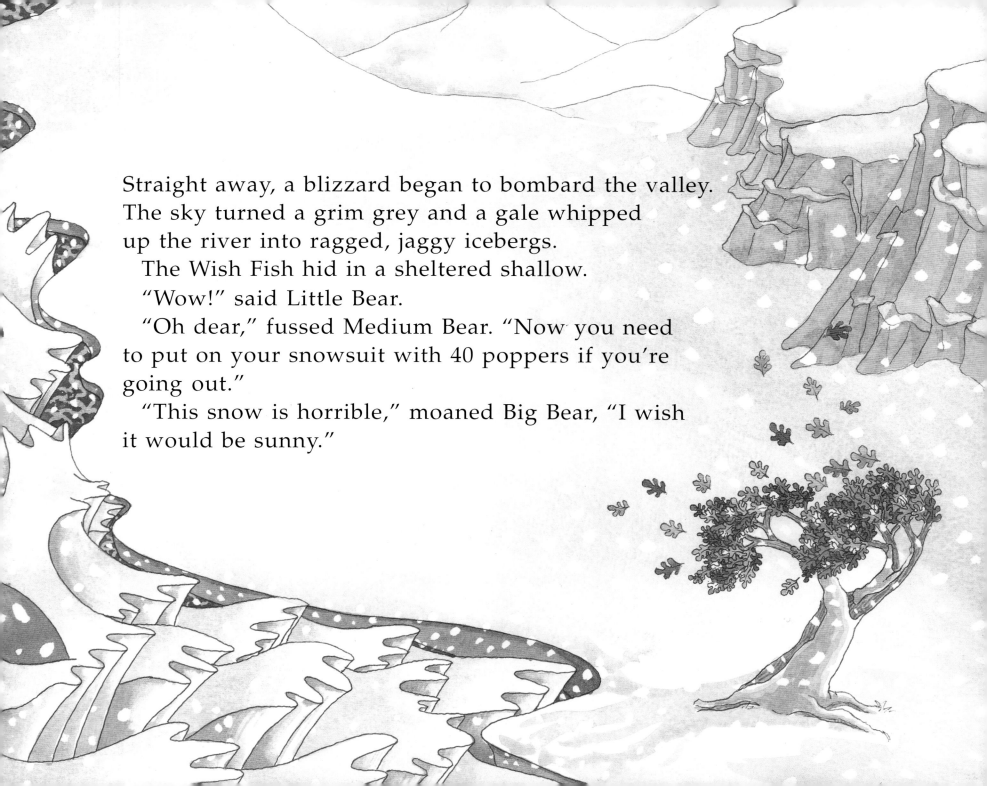

Straight away, a blizzard began to bombard the valley.
The sky turned a grim grey and a gale whipped
up the river into ragged, jaggy icebergs.

The Wish Fish hid in a sheltered shallow.

"Wow!" said Little Bear.

"Oh dear," fussed Medium Bear. "Now you need
to put on your snowsuit with 40 poppers if you're
going out."

"This snow is horrible," moaned Big Bear, "I wish
it would be sunny."

Immediately all the snow melted away and the grass
was singed brown. The river dried up to a muddy
trickle and the Wish Fish flipped and flopped in
a puddle outside the bear cave.

"Wow!" shouted Little Bear.

"And I'm so sticky," groaned Medium Bear, "I wish we lived in the Arctic Ocean."

Oh GLUB!

"I wish you two would stop moaning and leave me alone," said Little Bear crossly.

Oh HELP!

No sooner said than done.

   Little Bear found himself floating all alone
in the Arctic Ocean. There was nothing but water
and ice all around - not a Medium Bear or Big Bear
in sight.

Little Bear was miserable.
 "I'm cold and wet," he moaned.
 "I'm lonely," he moaned.
 "I wish ..."

The Wish Fish surfaced beside him.
  "Listen, kid," it said. "Get it right this time,
and no more moaning. One last wish and that's *it*."

Little Bear thought hard.
Waves slapped his muzzle.
He nearly wished that they wouldn't ...
but he stopped himself in time.

The ice froze his head into a furry popsicle.
He nearly wished for a woolly hat ...
but he stopped himself in time.

Little Bear wasn't a very good swimmer, and his fur was heavy. He began to sink.

He nearly wished for a life-jacket ... Then suddenly he knew what to wish for.

"I wish I lived in a cave by a river
with Big Bear and Medium Bear ...

and weather that snowed sometimes,
rained occasionally,
and was sunny more often than not."

And ... whoosh!

The bears of Papana River Valley
had their charmed life once more.
Big Bear's fur grew back eventually,
Medium Bear decided that the Arctic Ocean
was for polar bears, not cave bears,
and Little Bear taught them both
never to complain again,
because, after all,
life was peachy.

MORE PICTURE BOOKS IN PAPERBACK
FROM FRANCES LINCOLN

THE SNOWCHILD
Debi Gliori

Poor left-out Katie doesn't know how to play. She has lots of good ideas – but she's always out of step with the other children's games. Then, one winter's morning, Katie wakes up and decides to build a snowman...

Suitable for National Curriculum English – Reading, Key Stages 1 and 2
Scottish Guidelines English Language – Reading, Levels A and B

ISBN 0-7112-0894-8

COPY ME, COPYCUB
Richard Edwards
Illustrated by Susan Winter

Copycub learns everything by copying his mother.
A beautiful story alive with warmth and humour.

Suitable for National Curriculum English – Reading, Key Stage 1
Scottish Guidelines English Language – Reading, Level A

ISBN 0-7112-1460-3

MISSING!
Jonathan Langley

Every day, Lupin the cat is there to meet Daisy when she comes home from nursery. On the first day of the holidays, Lupin waits for Daisy as usual, but Daisy doesn't appear. Follow Lupin and Daisy's hilarious adventures as they set out to search for each other in this delightful and charmingly illustrated story.

Suitable for National Curriculum English – Reading, Key Stage 1
Scottish Guidelines English Language – Reading, Level A

ISBN 0-7112-1543-X

Frances Lincoln titles are available from all good bookshops.